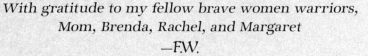

With gratitude to my fellow brave women warriors,
Mom, Brenda, Rachel, and Margaret
—F.W.

To my ama, Rosario Ang
—J.A.

Mulan: The Legend of the Woman Warrior
Text copyright © 2019 by HarperCollins Publishers
Illustrations copyright © 2019 by Joy Ang
www.harpercollinschildrens.com

Library of Congress Control Number: 2018934059
ISBN 978-0-06-280341-2

Typography by Erica De Chavez
19 20 21 22 23 SCP 10 9 8 7 6 5 4 3 2 1
❖
First Edition

Mulan

The Legend of the Woman Warrior

TRANSLATED FROM THE
CHINESE LANGUAGE BY
Faye-Lynn Wu

ILLUSTRATED BY
Joy Ang

HARPER
An Imprint of HarperCollinsPublishers

There once was a smart and strong-willed girl named Mulan, who lived in a small village in northern China with her parents, older sister, and younger brother.

One day, Mulan sat weaving, watching her
father pacing in the room. He looked old and frail.
She stopped. Turning to her father, she asked,
"Baba, what is worrying you?"

With a faraway look in his eyes, her father
replied, "I received a letter. The emperor has
called for all men to defend our country.
I must leave the family to join the army."

"How can you go? You are not well... and
Brother is far too young to go," Mulan said
with concern in her voice.

Mulan thought for a moment and then announced, "Baba, I can go in your place."

"How can you serve? You are only a girl," replied her father.

"I know I can. I am a strong and able girl," Mulan insisted.

The next day, Mulan, dressed in her father's clothes,
went to the market to buy a horse, a saddle, a bridle,
and a whip for the trip.

In the morning, Mulan bid farewell to her family.

When she arrived at the army camp, she and the troops set off for the north. Riding long miles, Mulan traveled to the Yellow River. At night she camped at the riverbank. Tired, Mulan dozed off to the sound of running water. She dreamed about her parents calling for her. "Mulan . . ." She missed her family.

Mulan rode on and traveled up to the top of Black
Mountain and settled across from the enemy's camp.

Exhausted, she fell asleep to the distant sound of the neighing horses. Again, Mulan dreamed about her parents calling her name. She missed her family even more. But she knew she was a strong and able girl. She was determined to work hard serving her country to make her family proud.

For twelve years, Mulan endured many hardships. She rode over
numerous mountain peaks and traveled thousands of miles on tired
legs. Often, she stayed awake through freezing nights.

Mulan fought in hundreds of battles
and led her comrades to many victories.

With her skills and bravery, Mulan rose quickly
through the ranks. As a victorious commander,
Mulan led her troops back to the emperor's palace.

The proud emperor beckoned the triumphant
troops to appear before him. Mulan was awarded
with countless pieces of gold and other treasures
for her courage and service.

The emperor praised Mulan and appointed her to the high court. The emperor asked Mulan what she might desire.

"Thank you, Emperor. I do not wish for the appointment to the high court. I only want to go back home to my family," Mulan replied.

The news of Mulan's return reached her family. To welcome her home, Mulan's parents eagerly waited at the outskirts of the town for her arrival. Her older sister was cheerfully dressing in her best outfit, while her younger brother was busily setting up for a feast. Upon arriving home, Mulan hugged her family.

She was happy to see them. She went to her room. She took off her armor and changed into her favorite dress. She sat down in front of her mirror, brushed out her tangled hair, and carefully applied color to her cheeks.

Mulan then rejoined her army buddies who were celebrating with her family in the living room. The men looked up at Mulan as she entered the room. With eyes wide open and a surprised look on their faces, they said in wonder, "How is it possible we did not know that our respected leader was a girl all along?"

Mulan smiled and responded, "One should not judge another by their appearance alone. When a pair of rabbits run side by side, can you tell the female from the male?"

Mulan continued, "A woman can fight any battle. Now I am happy once again to be just me, Mulan, a strong and able woman."

The Ballad of Mulan

唧唧復唧唧，木蘭當戶織。不聞機杼聲，惟聞女嘆息。
問女何所思？問女何所憶？女亦無所思，女亦無所憶。
昨夜見軍帖，可汗大點兵。軍書十二卷，卷卷有爺名。
阿爺無大兒，木蘭無長兄。願為市鞍馬，從此替爺征。
東市買駿馬，西市買鞍韉。南市買轡頭，北市買長鞭。

旦辭黃河去，暮宿黃河邊，不聞爺娘喚女聲，但聞黃河流水鳴濺濺。
暮宿黑山頭，不聞爺娘喚女聲，但聞燕山胡騎聲啾啾。

萬里赴戎機，關山度若飛。朔氣傳金柝，寒光照鐵衣，將軍百戰死，壯士十年歸。

歸來見天子，天子坐明堂。策勳十二轉，賞賜百千強。
可汗問所欲，木蘭不用尚書郎。願借明駝千里足，送兒還故鄉。

爺娘聞女來，出郭相扶持。阿姊聞妹來，當戶理紅妝。小弟聞姊來，磨刀霍霍向豬羊。
開我東閣門，坐我西閣床。脫我戰時袍，著我舊時裳。當窗理雲鬢，對鏡帖花黃。
出門看火伴，火伴皆驚惶。同行十二年，不知木蘭是女郎。
雄兔腳撲朔，雌兔眼迷離，兩兔傍地走，安能辨我是雄雌？